Third Grade ☆ MERMAid

Third Grade ⭐
MERMAID

Peter Raymundo

SCHOLASTIC PRESS/NEW YORK

Library of Congress Cataloging-in-Publication Data available

ISBN 978-0-545-91816-9

10 9 8 7 6 5 4 3 2 1   17 18 19 20 21

Printed in China   62
First edition, February 2017
Book design by Ellen Duda

This book is dedicated to Dorothy, Andrew, Billie, and Sugarloaf7, who inspired every page.

Monday

Today, we got our first report cards. And, if you ask me, I did ~~good great~~ GREAT! Better than great.

SHELLFISHALICIOUS GREAT! At least in what matters—

Like the 3 *S*'s!

Singing	A+
Swimming	A+
Splashing	A+

If I were my mother (and this was LAST YEAR), I'd be swimming backflips with joy! But **NOOO!** This isn't last year! And, for some crazy reason, in the third grade there's a FOURTH *S*. **Spelling!**

I've had to learn a new list of words every week! And even put the letters in the ~~rite riht~~ **RIGHT** order when I SPELL them! It's just CRAZY!

But I guess I didn't do so well a few times, because I got a great big **FISH** (minus the ish) on my report card!

So today when I got home from school, there was a strange little ~~tertus~~ ~~(tortoot~~ **TORTOISESHELL** book sitting on my bed.

The one I'm writing in right now!

And right beside it was

THIS! →

and THiS! →

OCTOPUS INK

Oohh!!! I should have known!

How ~~suspishus~~ **SUSPICIOUS** can you get? But silly me picked it up and started drawing when, **BAM**, my mother swims into my room with this big, fishy smile on her face!

Oh, I see you found your new diary.

"My new . . . what?"

"DIARY," my mother said, looking at my drawing. "You ~~kind right~~ WRITE in it . . . with words."

WORDS!

I knew this had something to do with that ~~redock riduckous~~ RIDICULOUS report card! "Well, if you think this so-called 'DIARY' is going to get me to write even a single word," I said with a laugh, "Ha ha ha! Boy are YOU wrong!"

My mother did a **hmph** sound, then flipped her tail to leave. "Have it your way," she said, "I was just trying to help."

"Help! Ha! You're just trying to trick me!" I yelled.

But then my mother twirled around and gave me her really SERIOUS face. The one with the squinty eyes. "Cora," she said, "I would never try to TRICK you."

"The diary," she said. "It's enchanted. And because you willingly put pen to paper, from now on you'll be compelled to write in it."

"Hold on a second!" I shouted. **"You put me UNDER A SSSPELL??"**

"It's funny you say that," Mother said, "because that's the whole point. Writing helps you S–P–E–L–L."

"And what's THAT supposed to mean?"

"My point exactly," she said. "But you'll see. Keeping a diary is good for you. Good for getting things out. Like your emotions."

My EMOTIONS? What EMOTIONS??? Why would I waste my time writing about my . . .

OHHHH! JUST SAYING THIS MAKES ME

So mad
I could just
SCREAM!

Oops. Sorry.

I just don't see how a worthless thing like spelling matters, anyway! I want to SWIM in the ocean, not WRITE about it!

~~Espe shelly~~ ESPECIALLY because I just made the **GREATEST, MOST POPULAR, MOST GLAMOROUS SWIM TEAM IN THE SEA—**

the singing sirens!

Well, the Jr. Sirens, actually. But we're all the same team! And practice starts TOMORROW for crying out loud! **TOMORROW!**

I bet the Sirens aren't worried about some stinking list of spelling words every week!

They're too busy being ~~bee-tu-tee buttiful~~ BEAUTIFUL!

I MEAN LOOK at her! →

When your scales have **THAT** much shine, who needs to spell?

If you ask me, Mother should be more worried about the huge lack of shimmer in my hair than some shrimp-sized F on a Report Card.

Splas**hy!**

Vol. 10010

12 SECRETS TO SHINIER SCALES!

Look GREAT at any DEPTH!

A look at the GREATEST, MOST POPU... MOST GLAMOROUS SWIM TEAM IN TH...

The SII GIN SI REN

Get the latest Bioluminescent Hair Wraps! pg. 32

Tuesday

Well, today is THE day! The first day of swim team practice! Eeeeee! School can't get done fast enough!

I can't believe I had to deal with all of those DIARY shellnanigans yesterday!

It doesn't matter! I can't get distracted and start doodling in this silly book again!

Now that I think about it, I better take this with me just in case Shelby starts sifting through my stuff again! (Little merbrothers can be so ANNOYING!)

Aaagh! I gotta go! I'm late for school! And now that I'm finally part of the swim team—

NOTHING! And I mean **NOTHING IS GETTING IN MY WAY!**

Aaargh! Thanks to that GIANT GROUPER, I bit my lip! AND nearly lost this book! But thank goodness I didn't! My mother would have been REALLY disappointed in me!

But besides that, today is art class! And the art teacher, Ms. Squid, is nice and all, but she only gives us one piece of stinkin' paper per class—

Because PAPER doesn't grow in the seas!

Well, class just started, and my ONE piece of paper is already RUINED!

We're supposed to do a watercolor portrait of our class partner, but MY class partner is a **JELLYFISH!**

"Focus on the lighting," Ms. Squid keeps saying, but how can I when the LIGHT goes right through him?

THIS is my messed-up painting of my friend Jimmy . . . the jellyfish. I actually wrinkled it up and threw it away, but then Ms. Squid UN-WRINKLED it and told me to keep going.

Jimmy the Jellyfish

And I would if Jimmy would just stop floating around!

Aaaaghh!!!

I just grabbed Jimmy's tentacle and tried to stop it from moving, and now **I CAN'T FEEL MY HAND!**

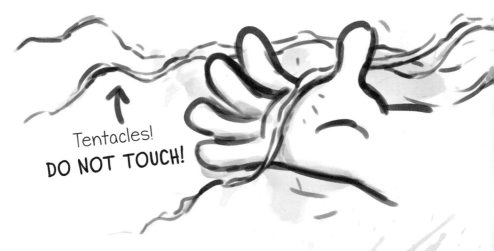

Tentacles!
DO NOT TOUCH!

And I've just spilled my paint! Why won't this class just end?

SHELLFISHALICIOUS! Class. Is. Over! But guess what? You know that picture of Jimmy that I almost threw away? Ms. Squid thought it was so good, she hung it up in front of the class!

And she gave me **THIS!**

(A golden starfish!)

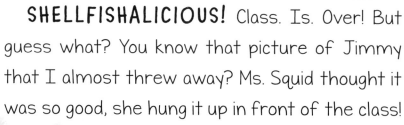

THESE are the paintings I did for the other kids in class once they knew I was an award-winning **ARTIST!**

Yep! Today must be my **LUCKY DAY!**

. . . or NOT!!

It's later now. I . . . I can hardly talk about what happened!

So I showed up for swim team practice after school, and right when I had gotten my official Singing Sirens swim cap snug on my head, Coach Finley dashed over and started **YELLING** at me!

Coach Finley

At first all I heard was "Bubble Bubble! Bu–Bubble Bubble!" So I thought it was just some kind of weird, bonefishy pep talk. But once his bubbles popped, I understood what he was saying!

You're off the team, Cora! Because of your GRADE!

Seriously! That's what he said!

I was so mad, I came home and threw my swim cap in the corner and swore I'd never wear it again!

Mother heard my screaming and yelling and swam into my room to "help." But when I told her I got kicked off the swim team because of my F in spelling, she got even madder than me!

Wednesday

Today my mother swam with me to school, and I can tell you, she was NOT happy!

Half the morning she argued with my teacher, Mr. Spouter, with her Squinty-Eyes on full blast. And I'm pretty sure Mr. Spouter wasn't happy either.

Then Coach Finley came in, and all four of us had to have a "talk," (INSTEAD OF GOING TO RECESS!) which made ME unhappy!

But at least some GOOD news came out of it. (Of course this was followed by BAD news, and then even WORSE news!)

The **GOOD** news is: I can get back on the swim team if I get an A on the next spelling test.

The **BAD** news is: I have to get an A on the next spelling test! And I have less than a WEEK to do it.

But wait! There's **WORSE** news! WAY worse!

Just when I thought the meeting was over, Coach Finley swims up and says if I **DON'T** pass the test, my spot will be taken by **VIVIAN SHIMMERMORE!**

YES! THE VIVIAN SHIMMERMORE!

How I beat Vivian out in the first place is a ~~never~~ ~~mirer-a-cal~~ **MIRACLE** I'll never understand. Although I did **SWIM** and **SPLASH** and **SING** with all my might!

Come to think of it, I don't think I EVER heard Vivian sing **A SINGLE NOTE!** Most of the time she just lounged around looking pretty.

Of course, that's where Vivian Shimmermore REALLY shines. Seriously, Vivian's skin is so perfect it actually shines (or "shimmers" as she likes to put it).

And, because of it, Vivian looks as amazing as her older sisters, and everyone knows it— including Vivian!

It's like, if you're pretty enough, you just get handed EVERYTHING, including a whole school of fish that follow every flip and flop of your fancy fins.

You should hear the little merboys when Vivian swims through a sunbeam.

"Oh, Vivian," they say, "your hair is so sparkly. And your SKIN! It's just so . . . so . . . perfect

it **GLOWS!**" And they're RIGHT! She does have everything, including my spot on the swim team! Aaagh!!!

HOW MUCH MORE DOES SHE WANT?

MUCH?
Um. Well, we were wondering if Vivian could borrow your swim cap.
If . . . you weren't using it.

HA!
THIS is my
official singing
sirens swim cap
that I've hidden
in this diary!
And will NEVER
give to Vivian
Shimmermore!
EVER!!!

Singing Sirens

Because I will be using it! All I have to do is learn that silly list of words they gave me. And how hard could **THAT** be?

drifted

toxic

species

predator

exoskeleton

ecosystem

Thursday

Aaaaaaghh!!! Very hard!

Look at that list! I can barely READ those words! Forget SPELLING THEM!

Eco-WHAT? What's THAT?!

There's no way those are third grade words! NO WAY!

Maybe I can just "sound them out."

Spee-shees Speacheaze

Aaagh! No good! I only covered the list for, like . . . THREE SECONDS and felt like my mind went BLANK!

There must be a secret to learning them or something. Hopefully some of my friends are **SMART** enough to tell me what it is!

Mother doesn't like me using my SHELL PHONE too much and all, but THIS is an **EMERGENCY!**

And I KNOW my best friend Sandy, who I've known for, like . . . EVER, will DEFINITELY help me out!

Later After WAY too much begging, Sandy and my other two best friends are coming over to help. I'd say Sandy is more of a SMART ALECK than anything else, but she's pretty good at laying out the facts when she needs to. And I have a feeling she might need to.

Now that I think about it, I'm pretty sure my other friend Jimmy doesn't actually have a brain. That's not an insult or anything. Jellyfish don't have brains. So I guess Jimmy floating over to help is a real no-brainer.

But thank goodness my THIRD friend, Larry the sea cucumber, isn't just smart, he's a GENIUS! (At least that's what he says.)

I know it gets pretty annoying when Larry starts talking all fancy, but at this point I'll listen to ANYTHING!

Sort of.

I just hope they get here soon, because there's only ONE thing I really want to know!

"The what?" Sandy giggled.

"The SECRET," I repeated, taking a deep breath of water, "to learning the words."

"Is this a trick question?" Jimmy asked.

"Perhaps," Larry said, "the only one Cora is tricking . . . is herself."

"What's wrong with you guys?" I yelled. "Why won't you just tell me the secret?"

"Because it's NOT a secret." Sandy chuckled.

"You just have to study," Jimmy added.

"STUDY? What's THAT?" I asked. "Some kind of algae?" And they laughed. LAUGHED! Because they thought I was joking.

But I guess the look on my face said I wasn't.

And that's when Larry started in with his smart talk.

"I believe the trouble you are having," he said, "is accepting a new reality."

"Ack—whating a new WHAT?"

"It means learning something new," Larry answered. "But it's a journey—the first step of which is **DENIAL**."

More like FINALLY he was done! I tell you, for having a mouth that faces the ground, that kid sure does talk a lot.

Look, Larry, I just want to move on.

"I cannot LOOK," Larry replied. "Sea cucumbers do not have eyes."

"WHAT???" I gasped.

"Then WHY do you always wear glasses?" Sandy laughed. But Larry wasn't laughing—at all.

WHAT GLASSES? Larry asked.

Like, he's TOTALLY off the **DEEP END!**

But I guess a few years ago somebody put those glasses on Larry as some kind of joke. And because he has no arms, Larry never reached up to know they were there!

Larry said he's sure it was one of the Sirens—that they've been flipping sand in his face for years.

When I said I found **THAT** hard to believe, Larry got really quiet.

I've got to say, though, I LIKE Larry's glasses. EVERYBODY does, including Larry. So he's going to keep wearing them, "Because they are IRONIC." (Whatever THAT means!)

ANYWAY! After my friends all left, I finally had to come face-to-face with my own new reality: **STUDYING**.

It turns out, though, studying is pretty simple. All you have to do is float in one spot for a while and STARE AS HARD AS YOU CAN.

It usually looks like **THIS:**

But for ME it looked like **THIS**:

I've never drifted off so fast in my life! And when I finally woke up from studying for three hours straight, I didn't feel smarter at all.

Here's the
DROOL to prove it!

Friday

What I really needed was INSPIRATION! And nothing inspires me more than stretching my fins with a nice, long SWIM!

But I guess I got TOO inspired, because today I just kept swimming and SWIMMING!

Until I ended up where I **REALLY** shouldn't be!

THE DUMPING ZONE! Where humans dump
their ~~toxic~~ ~~tocksick~~ TOXIC barrels of **SLUDGE!**

Mother says to NEVER go near them. And NEVER, **EVER** touch the slimy gook that comes out! She says the ocean is littered with the fish bones of those who have!

YUCK!

I shouldn't even be saying I was there! And I wouldn't if it wasn't for . . . ohhh! I'll get to that!

The fact is, I WAS there, okay? I didn't mean to be, but I was. And I was going to just leave when I saw him . . . it . . . **SOMETHING**, trapped under one of the barrels!

When I got closer, I saw it was a **SHRIMP**! A tiny, itsy-bitsy **SHRIMP**!

His tail was tucked under a barrel, and a bunch of glowing green sludge was about to ~~leke~~ ~~leek~~ **LEAK** all over him!

He needed my HELP!

And I don't care what ANYBODY says! There was **NO WAY** I was going to leave him there, toxic sludge or not!

So I swam right over . . .

and
PUSHED!

I pushed so hard, the shrimp came right out! But so did a bunch of stinky **SLUDGE**!

It was spilling right on top of him, so I grabbed the little guy by his tail and tried to shake him off.

And that's when I noticed he was
GLOWING!

The funny thing is, his glowing-ness helped me realize it was getting dark and I had to get home.

I couldn't remember exactly why, but I knew my mother is not very big on shrimp for some reason.

So I set him in a safe place and headed for home.

End of problem.

The thing about PROBLEMS, though, is SOMETIMES if you ignore them . . .

Then come looking for you!

And now I have a **GIANT SHRIMP** hiding in my bedroom! At the very least, he's not glowing anymore. But I just have to say, he **SMELLS**!

I'm sorry, but he does! Not bad, just . . . really, really **SALTY**!

Is that spelled right? I don't know. I doubt he can read this, anyway.

I just know it smells like a million SARDINES every time he leans up against me! Like he is RIGHT NOW!!

If I get licked in the face one more time, I might go crazy! But I do have to admit, having someone around to play with can be kind of fun.

I don't know if it's because of the toxic sludge or not, but Salty seems to learn things awfully fast for a shrimp!

We played games until it was time for bed, and I'm pretty sure most of the time I only won because he LET ME.

Saturday

This morning, I was dreaming of sitting on the rocks of a cove, singing, when a pesky **SEAGULL** flew down and started poking my shoulder with his BEAK!

"Cora. Cora," it kept saying. **"Wake up!"**

And eventually I did. When I opened my eyes, my **MOTHER** was sitting beside me, poking my shoulder!

Cora! Cora!

"Cora. Cora," she said. "Wake up. There's something wrong with your brother."

The first thing I thought was *DUHHH!* I've been saying THAT for years!

But Mother wasn't joking! Normally, my brother's face (although completely annoying) looks something like—

But today it looked more like **THIS:**

"I don't understand it," Mother said. "The last time this happened was when we found out your brother is allergic to SHELLFISH."

"Allergic to **SHELLFISH**?" I blurted. "You mean like . . . SHRIMP?"

"Yes!" Mother said, "Like shrimp and crabs and lobsters and . . . and . . ."

Anything with an **exoskeleton.**

"An EX–SO–WHAT?" I said.

"An exoskeleton." Shelby wheezed. "E–X–O–S–K–E–L–E–T–O–N."

"I can spell your silly word, Shelby!" I moaned. (Of course, I couldn't, but I wasn't about to tell HIM that.)

Mother frowned. "Cora, you haven't seen any little shrimp around here, have you? Those little buggers can hide ANYWHERE."

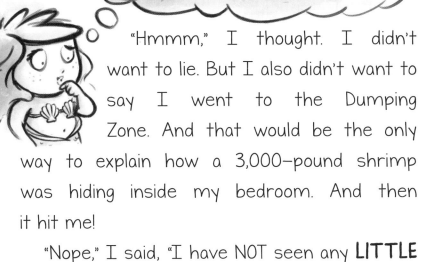

"Hmmm," I thought. I didn't want to lie. But I also didn't want to say I went to the Dumping Zone. And that would be the only way to explain how a 3,000-pound shrimp was hiding inside my bedroom. And then it hit me!

"Nope," I said, "I have NOT seen any **LITTLE** shrimp around here."

Mother was about to speak, but I cut her off.

"Absolutely no teeny-weeny, itsy-bitsy, little shrimp at all," I said. "No. Small. Shrimp. Period."

"Okay, Cora. I heard you," Mother said. "Now, listen. Your brother and I need to go see Dr. Beluga to get some of that kelp cream he used last time."

Dr. Beluga

Kelp Cream

"Ummm. Okay," I shrugged. But she was acting weird. I thought for sure Mother knew about the shrimp but wasn't saying it.

"So I'm assuming you want to stay home?" Mother asked and said at the same time.

Well, I guess so. **Why?**

"To STUDY!" Mother exclaimed. "You only have a few days left until your test. As far as I can tell, you've barely studied at all."

"Oh! The TEST." I laughed. "Right. Ha ha! But I have studied."

"She means with your eyes OPEN." Shelby smirked. He was trying to make me mad, as usual. But by that point I had bigger things on my mind. MUCH BIGGER!

That was an hour ago. I think my mother WAS worried and wouldn't have left if it wasn't totally necessary. But it was. So she did.

And now I'm here alone . . . with the shrimp.

The thing is, I **DO** have to study, but CAN'T! Because Salty the Shrimp here keeps dropping this old stick of coral on my book! Then every time I throw it, he brings it right back and drops it again!!!

And I can tell you, SHRIMP SLOBBER is disgusting!

shrimp slobber

I wish I could just throw that stick and make it keep going! Like that time I fooled Shelby into chasing a—

HOLD ON A SECOND!

I have an IDEA!

Later

I'm so tired now I can barely keep my eyes open.

Like I said, Salty kept wanting me to throw some slobbery stick of coral just so he could bring it back—right when I was trying to study! It was maddening!

So I had this IDEA to tie the piece of coral to one of those super-fast tunas, so when I threw it, the shrimp would just keep going and going.

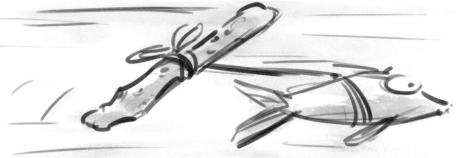

I figured it would be just like Larry says: "Out of sight. Out of mind." At least, that was my plan.

So I swam out as far as I could, leading
Salty with his "stick." I tried not being seen,
but that's pretty much IMPOSSIBLE when
a whale-sized shrimp is swimming right
behind you!

But, anyway, after I got as far out as
I dared go, I grabbed hold of that stick—
and **THREW**!

The tuna took off with the stick! And Salty took off after him!

But right as they were too far away to see, I wished I had never thrown it at all.

I mean, "Out of sight. Out of mind," might be great when you have homework, but it's horrible when you're losing a friend.

Larry also says: "Sometimes you don't know what you've got till it's gone."

Good-bye, Salty.

No one else ever followed me around or licked my face or brought back a stick when I threw it. And probably no one ever would again.

I started swimming back home to study, feeling sad and alone in more ways than one!

When Salty was beside me, I didn't see a single killer whale or mermaid–eating shark. But now that I was by myself, the ocean seemed full of them!

When I'm really sad, though, I just want to be left alone. So when a gang of sharks started circling me, I was definitely NOT in the mood—especially when I saw who it was!

They call themselves **the Razor Tooths**, which is just . . . oh come on! Razor TOOTHS? Why not TEETH or TEETHS or TOOTH, even! It's just so annoying!

But even MORE annoying is their so-called leader, Magilla. He's a rare ~~spee~~ ~~spea~~ **SPECIES** of **"not-so-great" white shark**. The kind with a big mouth and even bigger appetite.

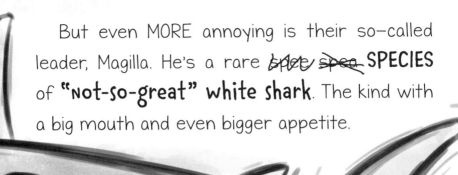

Not-so-greats are just as deadly as the great kind, of course. They're just not as smart because they dropped out of shark school.

But just because Magilla's not a great white SHARK doesn't mean he's not a GREAT BIG BULLY!

He wasn't even funny. Obviously. But all his little followers just laughed and laughed to fit in.

The thing is, all bullies like Magilla ever want is respect. Or food. Or both. And I didn't feel like giving him either.

Magilla stopped mid-laugh, looking confused.

"It means For Your Information," a pilot fish blurted. "She's being snotty, sir."

"Um. Technically, I think she's right, though," the lemon shark added. "It WOULD be difficult to, well . . . see her eyes get watery because we are, in fact—"

Aaah! SHUT your blabbering gills, you!

I'm not caring about filling my brain with IN-FOR-MA-TION.

"But my stomach," Magilla said with a snarl, "I have no trouble filling at all."

Then he SMILED, ~~another thing~~ UNSHEATHING his razor-sharp teeth. But no matter how frightening and horrible Magilla's toothy grin was, his **BREATH WAS WORSE!**

Eewww! You have been eating **SARDINES!**

And I thought your **JOKES** were bad!

And, believe it or not, the other sharks started **LAUGHING!**

HA HA HA HA She does have a point!

If there's one thing a bully REALLY hates, it's being bullied. So I figured I better smooth things out pretty quickly.

And I did.

"Oh, I'm just kidding, Magilla," I said in my sweetest voice. "Your jokes ARE good. I promise."

They ... they are?

Boy, was he desperate for a compliment! One more and I would have been off the hook. But then I thought about how rude Magilla was and just couldn't help myself.

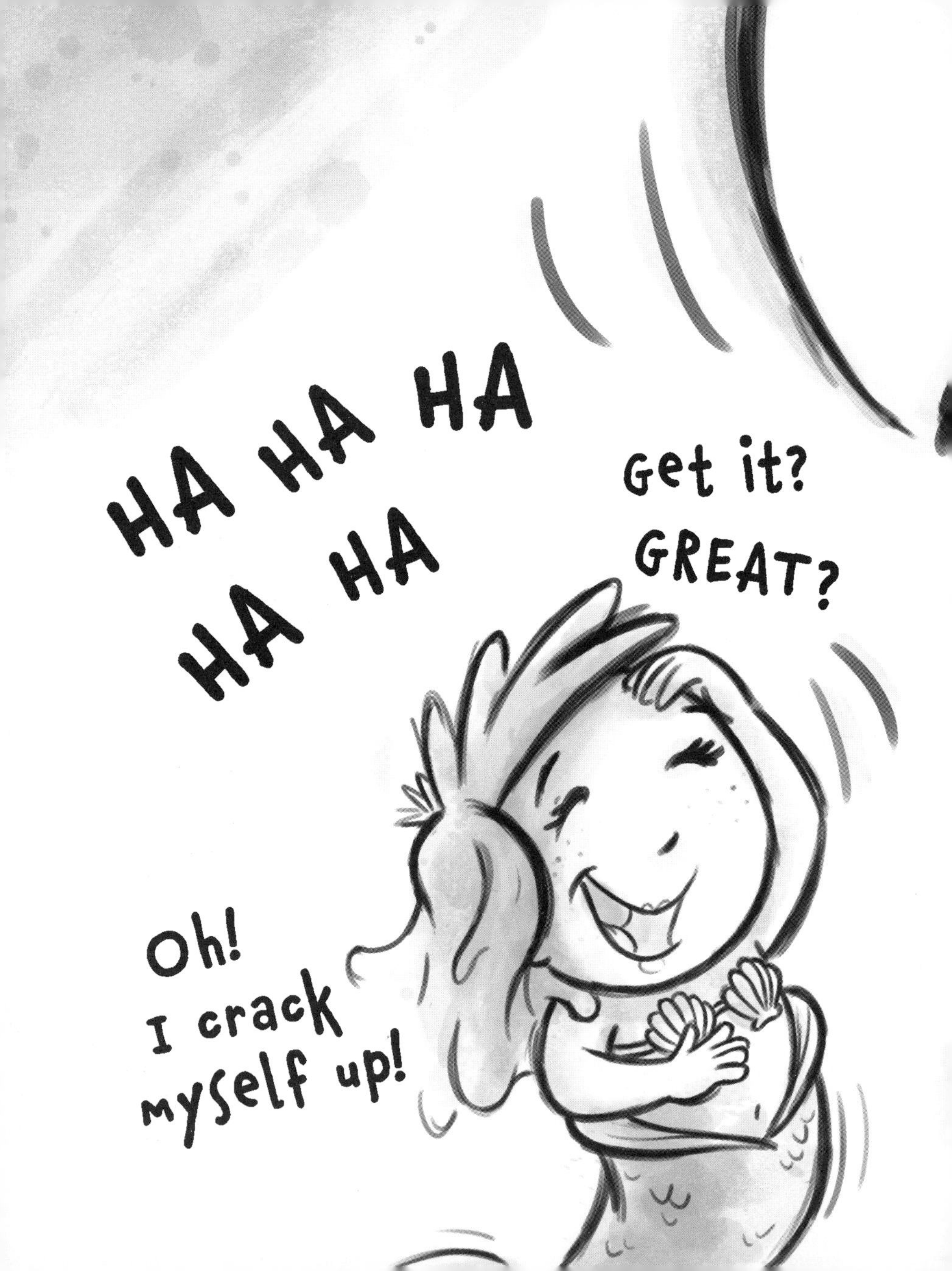
HA HA HA
HA HA
Get it? GREAT?
Oh!
I crack myself up!

Talk about rubbing a shark the wrong way!

Luckily, I've dealt with this before!
And there's one thing I've learned about
bully sharks!

They might be BIG and
STRONG and HUNGRY . . .

But they're really
easy to FOOL!

MOST of the time!

The fact was, I was trapped and about to become mermaid sushi—

When something **AMAZING** happened!

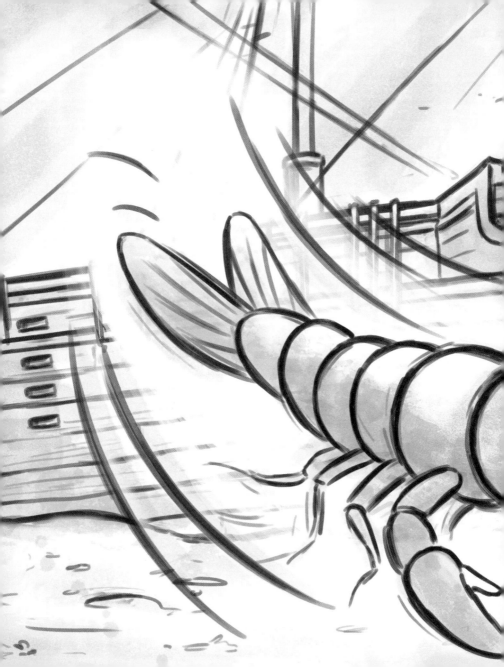

SNAP!

It was **SALTY!**

He came back just in time!

And I can say this much: If Magilla felt bad about not being called "great," he must have felt HORRIBLE getting beat up by a shrimp!

And talk about feeling horrible! I could hardly face Salty after how I tricked him. I said I was sorry, and I truly was.

When Salty turned around to face me I could tell he wasn't mad.

Then he tossed me his stick, slobber and all, and I knew everything was okay.

After all that, I finally made it back home, having accomplished absolutely nothing. I still had a giant shrimp following me around, and I STILL hadn't studied my spelling words . . . AGAIN!

So I took out my list and tried to at least read it over. I must have been super-tired from my whole adventure, though, because I don't even remember falling asleep.

But I sure remember waking up! I didn't even know that my mother's face could make THAT expression!

Mother's expression
(too crazy to show!)

Obviously I had a **TON** of explaining to do. (Actually, I think Salty weighs a **ton and a half**, but I didn't want to embarrass him.)

I could tell that my story seemed like one big fish tale, but they kind of HAD to believe me because Salty was sitting right there as proof.

I guess the way I told it must have worked, though. Mother didn't like that I hid Salty from her, but she WAS proud that I rescued a creature in need.

Shelby wasn't as easy to convince. Dr. Beluga's cream might have fixed Shelby's face, but it didn't do much for his personality.

"A new WHAT? But I don't want a **PET**!" I yelled.

Then Mother said that having a pet might teach me some ~~reaspoon~~ RESPONSIBILITY!

"But I don't want THAT either!"

"Of course you don't, dear," Mother said. Then she and Shelby swam out of my room. The worst part was Shelby leaving with that smug look on his face.

So here I am. Alone with the shrimp and that spelling list . . . AGAIN! But this time, I'm going to study those words no matter what! AARRGH!! Gimme that list!

Word One: Drifted

D

Sunday

Well, this morning I woke up with my spelling list covered in drool and stuck to my face . . . AGAIN!

How did I even get in this mess?

I clearly know nothing about spelling, and even less about having a pet.

But WAIT! I know who DOES know about pets! Sandy! She had that parrot fish for years. He was cute and all, except he kept repeating the same jokes again and again.

It doesn't matter, though. Sandy had a pet, and maybe she can give me some advice about mine.

I do NOT know why Sandy thinks that is so funny!

Anyway, when I finally got to telling her about Salty, I realized she would really have to see him to understand. I told her to get Jimmy and Larry together and come over.

But then Sandy gave me a hard time about having to go somewhere with her parents and Blah! Blah! Blah! She said I'd have to come all the way to HER part of the ocean if I wanted to meet for FIVE MINUTES!

FIVE MINUTES?

Wait until you see what I have!

Well, I didn't make it in four minutes. Or five minutes! Or AT ALL for that matter! All because I tried to take a "shortcut" through Old Rocky Cove.

(Of course I wouldn't have if Sandy hadn't rushed me in the first place!)

But, anyway, I did. And when I was going by, I saw some mermaids lounging up on the rocks. And I could tell by their tails they weren't just any old mermaids! They were Sirens! They had to be!

So I tied Salty's leash to an old anchor and went to see what was going on.

And when I came up to the surface, I saw they were Sirens all right!

The Singing Sirens!

They were practicing their newest songs and looking **GLAMOROUS AS EVER!**

I would have left after a minute, but guess who ELSE was there!

Vivian Shimmermore!

Yes! THE Vivian Shimmermore!

I guess I got so disgusted seeing Vivian hanging out with the Sirens that I forgot she was one! So, without thinking, I swam over and actually got up in that shimmering face of hers.

Vivian rolled over and lifted one of her painted-on eyelashes like it weighed a ton. Then she just shut it again without even looking at me once!

"Can you move to the left?" she breathed. "You're blocking my sun."

Aaaargh! The classic close-your-eyes-while-you're-speaking technique! And the sad part is . . . IT WORKED!

"Oh, sorry," I said and moved out of the way. But then I thought, *that's not HER sun*! And moved right BACK in the way!

This, at least, got Vivian annoyed enough to look at me when she spoke.

I'm here with my sisters! What's the big deal?

I didn't have to look over, of course, Vivian Shimmermore's sisters **ARE** a big deal. The BIGGEST deal.

Arabella and Belinda Shimmermore are not only Singing Sirens; their perfect voices and practically GLOWING skin have made them the most famous and glamorous mermaids this side of the equator!

They even wrote a book in case you had any questions!

So, it's not like I forgot that Vivian was related to world-famous Sirens or anything. I just ignored it.

I was about to tell Vivian if she hadn't lucked into the same extra-shimmery skin her sisters had, that she wouldn't be HALF as popular. But all of a sudden, Vivian's oldest sister, Arabella, burst through the water beside us!

She propped herself up on the rocks with both hands, then whipped her hair back in one, glorious motion. Up close, her skin was even more . . . "GLOWY" than Vivian's.

"And who is this?" Arabella asked in that high-pitched voice she's so famous for.

"My name's Cora," I said, reaching my hand out to shake hers. "It's an honor to meet you."

Arabella looked down at me and sighed.

Sirens. Don't. Shake.

"Oh, sorry," I said and pulled my hand back down.

"This is Cora," Vivian said, "the mermaid I told you about. The one with that spelling test deal. You know."

And Arabella DID seem to know. "Oh, yes, Corrrr—a," Arabella purred. "And how's it going? This . . . learning to ssssspell?"

"Actually, really good," I said. "I'd say I'm going to pass that test for sure."

Suddenly Vivian perked up nervously . . .

But HOW? You haven't passed a spelling test all year.

Well, I guess I'm just studying. You know.

Arabella **LAUGHED** out loud!

Angelfish, the only "studying" I know about...

are **THOSE** sailors...

studying **THIS** face...

until they hit **THOSE** rocks...

And as if she timed it herself, another Siren yelled out, "A ship is coming! Get to your spots!"

Arabella's eyes grew black with excitement. "Stay here," she said, "It's SHOWTIME."

Arabella joined her older teammates on the edge of the cove. Just as a big fishing boat came over the horizon, the Sirens began to sing.

**"Listen. Listen," the Sirens sung.
"The rocks, they are your friends."**
I thought I noticed Vivian just mouthing the words, but it was hard to tell. The other Sirens' voices completely filled the air, practically steering the fishing boat right toward them.

I never thought I'd say this, but I felt kind of bad for those fishermen. They were headed ~~STRATE~~ STRAIGHT for their doom but were so focused on the Sirens' song, they couldn't think of anything else.

And when they got close enough to actually see the Sirens themselves, there was REALLY no turning back.

Or at least **THAT'S WHAT I THOUGHT!**

But right as the boat was about to smash into the rocks, one of the sailors yelled out, **"SEA MONSTER!"**

The Singing Sirens dove out of sight as the sailors grabbed their FISHING SPEARS to throw. But the men weren't aiming at the Sirens. They were aiming at ME!

I was so shocked. I turned around to see if they might be pointing at something else, and **THEY WERE**!

Eeeeeeeeee!

It was **SALTY**! He'd come looking for me and had brought the anchor he was tied to with him!

A metal spear whizzed past my ear! Then one nearly hit Vivian!

"Vivian! Get down!" I yelled. But she was scared stiff! So I grabbed Vivian's clammy hand and pulled her to safety under the water.

I tried to ask Vivian if she was hurt, but she was more scared of Salty than of the sailors.

"Vivian, it's okay!" I yelled. But it was too late. She pushed me into Salty and swam off as fast as she could.

After everything calmed down, though, I remembered why I was going through Old Rocky Cove in the first place!

SANDY!

I was SUPPOSED to meet her, Larry, and Jimmy a long time ago! And if there is one thing Sandy does **NOT** joke about, it's being **LATE!**

I swam as fast as a sailfish to Sandy's part of the reef!

everyone was gone.

I did find Larry's trail in the sand, though, and figured I could just follow it to where he was.

But, after a while, Larry's trail crossed with some OTHER sea cucumber's path.

Then those paths crossed another, and ANOTHER! And before long, the sea floor looked more tangled than my hair!

So I just swam home. The **LONG WAY**.

I'm sure I'll see Sandy and the others in school tomorrow. I just hope they're not TOO mad at me for not showing up.

Monday

THIS is what greeted me at school.

I tell you, those so-called "friends" of mine really made me SWEAT! And that's not easy for a mermaid.

I told them I was sorry for being late, and that something REALLY, REALLY important came up, but they all just kept giving me the ol' fish eye!

"You've got to be JOKING!" I yelled. But before I could say any more, they burst out LAUGHING!

"**RELAX**," Sandy said, "We **ARE** joking! Geez!"

"You should see the look on your face," Jimmy added. "You look like you just ate a bad piece of monkfish or something! It's hilarious!"

"Yes. It is quite humorous," Larry said.

Yeah, real funny.

Obviously it WASN'T. But I was so relieved to be off the hook, I tried to act like nothing ever happened.

Until something DID happen!

It was **VIVIAN SHIMMERMORE** herself! Picking the absolute WORST TIME EVER to start being friendly!

"I see you are still alive?" Vivian said in that uppity tone of hers.

"Um . . . yes?" I answered.

"Hm–hmm. Well, I just wanted to say I appreciate you . . . helping me yesterday."

"Oh, don't mention it." I laughed, wishing she'd just go away!

I wouldN't. But my sisters insisted I invite you to my birthday party. It's tomorrow night.

"Presents are required," she added.

Then Vivian just swam away, leaving me with nothing but her fancy invitation and a whole lot to explain.

"Guilty of WHAT?" I yelled. "So I got sidetracked by the Sirens on my way over, okay? They're really not so bad, you know."

But we waited for you, Cora.

Don't you even care?

"Of course I do," I said. "I said I was sorry. I just didn't want to tell you why because you guys wouldn't understand."

"Understand what?" Sandy laughed. But it was kind of an angry laugh.

"The Sirens' song," I said. "You guys have never heard it. It's just . . . beautiful."

"Wow," Larry muttered, "I think someone drank too much seawater."

Cora, listen, you are so blinded by Vivian Shimmermore and her big-tail sisters . . .

it's like you can't see anything else!

"Like WHAT?" I spat.

"Like REALITY," Sandy said.

"Oooo . . . that was good," Larry whispered. And that was all I could take.

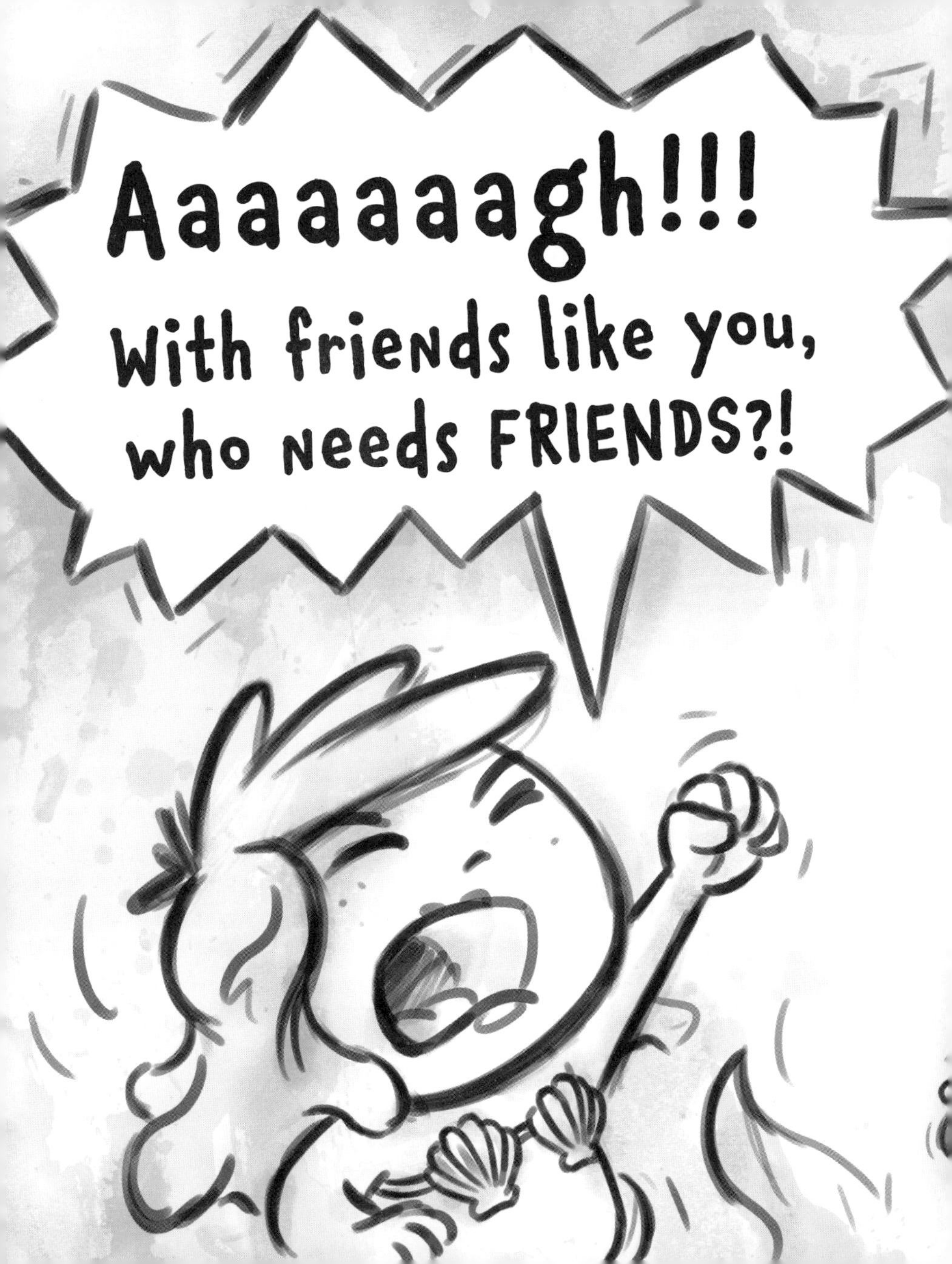
Aaaaaaaagh!!!
With friends like you, who needs FRIENDS?!

Tuesday

I tell you, my luck goes up and down like the tides. I woke up early thinking I have just one more day until that spelling test and I haven't learned a single word!

drifted

toxic

species

predator

exoskeleton

ecosystem

Just to prove it, I tried "studying" again, but found out something **AMAZING**! I could spell almost every word AND knew what they meant! I guess this diary really does have a **SPELL** on it.

But the real reason I got up early was our class field trip to the Giant Kelp Forest. I've been looking forward to it for months. This time of year, we go there to collect sea urchins because those little guys eat too much of the kelp.

Mr. Spouter says the kelp needs to be protected—that it's important for a healthy ~~echo~~ ~~eeeko~~ ECOSYSTEM. (I guess that means everything living together nicely.)

The funny thing is, Mr. Spouter is the only one in the class who can't breathe underwater. So every couple of hours he has to keep going up to the surface for a "breathing break."

When he leaves, Mr. Spouter always says the same thing too: Stick with your buddyfish and **DON'T GET LOST!**

But as Larry says, "When the whale is away, the fish will play." And sure enough, when Mr. Spouter was up at the surface, some wahoo named Peto ended up getting lost in the forest.

I've got my buddy.

I've got mine!

Hey! Where's Peto?

So then the rest of us had to go look for him without getting lost ourselves!

Of course, I went with Larry. He may not have eyes, but that guy ALWAYS knows where he's going. "Because others may look, but do not see," he said. But that's right when things REALLY went **DOWNHILL**!

She was gulping down kelp like there was no tomorrow! And Mr. Spouter thought the sea urchins were bad!

When Vivian heard me, she spit out her evidence and spun around to face us.

"Looks like someone's been caught with their hand in the cookie jar," Larry said.

What's a cookie jar?

"This doesn't prove **ANYTHING!**" Vivian pouted, pointing her nose in the air.

It proves you like chlorophyll.

"Ha! I don't like Clara OR Phil!" Vivian laughed.

"I said CHLOROPHYLL." Larry groaned. "In KELP it helps absorb energy from the sun. And when eaten by average-looking mermaids, like our friend here, it gives her skin that 'GLOW' she's so famous for. But it's **FAKE.**"

"Look here, you little sea slug," Vivian said with a snarl. "Maybe I do use a little help with 'GLOW,' as you call it. But at least I'm not UGLY."

As Vivian turned to go, she flipped SAND in Larry's face. Larry said nothing, but I'd seen enough!

"YOU'RE the UGLY one, Vivian!" I yelled, "You're not even nice at all! You just go around acting like you're better than everyone else because your sisters are famous Sirens."

But guess what?

YOU are NOT!

Vivian spun back around and glared at me with those cold blue eyes of hers.

"You," Vivian growled, "I don't care what my sisters' plan was. YOU are not invited to my party anymore!"

Her PARTY? THAT'S all she had to say? I thought she couldn't get any more shallow!

But then Vivian leaned in so close I could smell her kelpy breath. "Unless," she said, sneering, "you bring a REALLY . . . GOOD . . . **PRESENT.**"

Ha! What a joke that girl is! I wouldn't give her a present if she had the last birthday on earth!

I wish everyone just KNEW Vivian was eating the very kelp we're SUPPOSED to be protecting, just so she can "SHIMMERMORE!"

Aaagh! It wouldn't even matter! No one would even care! Except . . . the SIRENS! THEY would care! Their beauty is REAL! And I bet they'll be ~~furry furry~~ FURIOUS to find out what a cheater Vivian is. I just wish there was a way I could tell them all at once.

But WHEN? And WHERE?

You are invited to
Vivian Shimmermore's
Birthday Party!

When: Tuesday night!   **Where: The Old Ship Graveyard**

Presents are REQUIRED.

Oh yes! Yes! Yes! Yes!

Why didn't I think of that before? I bet ALL of the Sirens will be there. Oh man! This is my chance!

I bet when I tell the Sirens what a ~~phone~~ ~~foney~~ PHONY Vivian is, they're going to BEG me to be on the team!

But first, I need to get ready! Tonight, I need to look as GOOD AS POSSIBLE!

Comb my hair!

Shine my fins!

And oh yeah! Mother let me borrow her PEARL NECKLACE!

She actually said I could keep it if I wanted, but told me I looked perfectly beautiful without it. I'm not sure if THAT'S true or not, but I am sure I'm going to need every ounce of "shim" I can get just to fit in.

Okay! I'd better go! I'm sure I'll be writing about my **FUN** and **SUCCESSFUL** night when I get back!

Later

Well, I'm back. Luckily. And I don't think ANYONE would call tonight "FUN," but I guess in some ways I'd call it a success.

It's funny, too. I started off in such a hurry to get there, hoping nothing would mess up my plan.

I even snuck out of the reef as quietly as I could just in case Salty wanted to follow me. A lot of good that did me, though.

I know Salty was just trying to keep me safe. But I had to explain that if HE kept saving me, I'd never learn to save myself.

Just saying that, I felt like I'd been hanging out around Larry too long. But it worked. Salty looked sad, but seemed to understand. And let me go.

Not surprisingly, Vivian's party was at the Old Ship Graveyard. It's a pretty neat place and all, but I don't go there very much. When I do, it always feels like I'm swimming around in Vivian's backyard or something.

The Shimmermores don't own it, of course, but if you ever talk with Vivian about it, you'd think they did.

She just LOVES to brag about how her great-granny Shimmermore was "the very first Siren to sink a ship there. And every generation of Shimmermores have added to it ever since."

Of course, somehow Vivian always leaves out that SHE hasn't sunken anything yet.

The actual party was on a sunken whaling ship that once chased Mocha Dick himself. In fact, the entrance was through a hole the shape of the giant whale head.

HAPPY BIRTHDAY VIVIAN!

Of all the boats in the graveyard, that probably wasn't the best one to have a party on. Of course, I might just be saying that because I know what happened later.

I have to admit, though, they really went all out with the decorating.

Usually no one has parties at night because it's too dark. But Vivian's parents must have lured in every ~~biolloam~~ ~~bylee~~ **BIOLUMINESCENT** squid, fish, and jellyfish they could find just to light the place up!

And right in the center of it all was Vivian Shimmermore, sparkly as ever, sitting beside the biggest **Underwater Lava Cake** I have ever seen!

Actually, I could only see the top of it because so many people and presents were in the way!

"Hey!" someone yelled. "The line starts over there!"

"What line?" I asked. Then I realized most of the guests were standing in a line as long as the boat!

"The GIFT line!" someone else grumbled.

I found it disgusting that Vivian had a "gift line" at all. And FUNNY that I didn't even bring one!

"Hey, Cora," another voice called out.

"Okay! I'll move, for crying out loud!" But when I spun around, I couldn't believe who it was!

It was Jimmy! And Sandy! And Larry!

"We came to support you," Sandy said. "That's what friends are for."

"Yeah, but . . . how did you even know I was here? Or why?"

"And read," Larry said. "And apparently you're quite a writer."

"What? My PET has been reading my diary?"

The thought of it sent a chill up my fish bones, but that didn't make me half as chilly as the voice I heard coming from behind me.

"What are YOU doing here?"

It was Vivian Shimmermore, of course. The Singing Sirens were right behind her like some kind of mermaid gang.

"And besides the fact that you've come empty-handed," she said, "that invitation was just my sisters' idea of a joke."

Oh, no, she didn't! But she DID! Vivian Shimmermore made fun of the fanciest thing my mother ever gave me.

"Oh yeah?" I said, "Well, maybe the Sirens would like to know your little secret, Vivian."

Vivian sighed. "And what shocking 'secret' would that be, Cora?"

"That Vivian here," I said, looking at the Sirens, "secretly eats kelp to get her 'shimmer.'"

There was total silence. The Sirens were shocked all right—that I thought this was a secret!

"You see," Vivian said, "**ALL** the Sirens eat kelp and just blame it on those little sea urchins. Isn't that funny?"

Obviously, I didn't think it was. But judging by the smirks on the Sirens' faces, THEY certainly did. Because it was true.

"Let's just go," Sandy said. "Vivian wouldn't know funny if it smacked her in the face."

Then all of a sudden came a *BOOM!* And this huge chunk of CAKE flew in and **SMACKED** Vivian right in the face!

SPLAT!

It was Vivian's **Underwater Lava Cake!**
They built it on top of an actual underwater
VOLCANO! And with all the **PRESENTS** piled up
next to it, the hole got plugged, and caused it
to BLOW!

CAKE and PRESENTS flew everywhere!
But so did **REAL LAVA!** Everyone started
pushing and shoving to get out of there!

I picked up Larry and tossed him over to
Sandy. "Go! I'll catch up!" I yelled. Then I
turned back to try to help Jimmy but saw that
he'd already floated to safety.

Relieved, I turned BACK around to get out of there, but then my NECKLACE got twisted on the wet bar!

I couldn't budge!

And the mermaids I was trying to impress only moments before just left me there to get swallowed up by Vivian's cake.

Just like the sailors on that fishing boat, I was so blinded by the Singing Sirens' beauty that I couldn't see anything else. And now I was trapped by a necklace I wore just to impress them.

THEY'RE *the sea monsters*, I thought, *not Salty.* Because he's just himself, and that's the most BEAUTIFUL thing you can be!

And that's when I realized I didn't even need that necklace anymore!

In fact, I NEVER needed it. So I grabbed a hold of those pearls and . . .

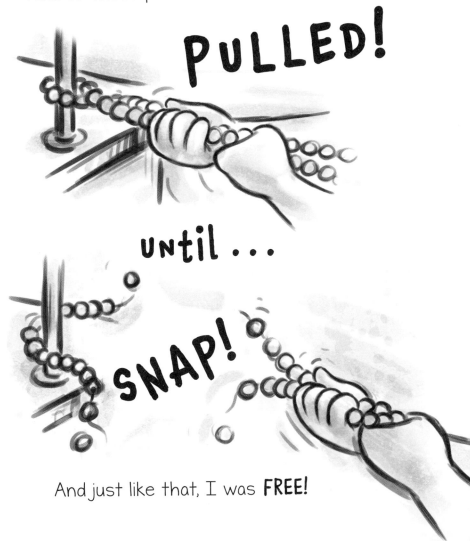

PULLED!

until . . .

SNAP!

And just like that, I was **FREE!**

Outside of the Old Ship Graveyard, everyone gathered to watch the volcano swallow up the whaling ship we were just on.

"Congratulations, Vivian," I said. "I bet you're the very first Shimmermore to sink a ship that was already sunk." And to my great ~~satisfakshun~~ satisfaction, the Sirens laughed.

When I got back home, Mother and Shelby had already heard about "the exploding cake incident." In fact, they HEARD the explosion, because sound travels fast underwater.

I was kind of scared to tell Mother what happened to the pearl necklace she gave me, but she wasn't mad at all.

Mother said she was just happy I made it home in one piece **(which is more than I can say for Vivian's birthday presents).**

I better go to sleep now. Tomorrow is the big day. The spelling test. I tell you, this week has already been one for the books. Well, at least one book—my diary.

It's almost full now, but Mother DID get it to help me with the test, so I guess that's not a bad way to end it.

wednesday

This whole week has been one big TO-DO. I've had to do things I DIDN'T want to do, just to do something I wanted to do!

The crazy part is, the thing I was **FORCED** to do became the thing I **WANTED** to do!

I tell you, it felt **SHELLFISHALICIOUS** to swim into school this morning and take that spelling test knowing I was ready.

And it felt even BETTER when I got the test back!

You know you've done something great when half the class thinks you cheated and the other half wants to know your secret.

But how could I explain? I did more than just sit there and study the words, I used them to tell my own story. Better than that, I LIVED them.

Name: Cora M.
Teacher: Mr. S

Spelling Test

1. exoskeleton
2. drifted
3. species
4. toxic
5. predator
6. ecosystem

A⁺

After school, Coach Finley was ready to welcome me back to the team, but I told him it just didn't interest me anymore and Vivian could have my spot. (But NOT my swim cap!)

Coach Finley was so shocked, he almost swallowed his whistle! But I heard that Vivian was so relieved at the news, she almost cried. Of course I find THAT hard to believe.

Then, when I came home, I told Mother my decision, and she said she was happy with it, as long as I was. And I am.

But wait. There's more! **WAY** more!

Mother said to stay put, then quickly swam over to the other side of the reef. When she came back, she had the big, fishy smile she gets when she's up to something.

She said she was so proud of me for making such a big decision, then asked if I had used the diary she gave me to figure things out.

I thought this was one of the craziest questions she ever asked. "Ever use it?" I exclaimed, "I could never NOT use it, thanks to that **SPELL** it put me under!"

At this my mother raised an eyebrow. "What spell is that?" she asked.

"Oh, come on!" I said, grabbing the diary and flipping it open. "This spell! The spell that forced me to love writing so much I filled this entire book in a week!"

But guess what?

I'm on the last page.

So it looks like my writing days are done! End of Story!

I slammed the book shut for emphasis.

Mother just stared at me, then the book, then at me. Then she laughed!

"Cora," she said, "there IS no spell. I thought you knew I was joking."

"WHAT??? What are you talking about?!"

"You love drawing because you're good at it," Mother said, "and writing because it's fun!"

"**HOLD ON A SECOND!**" I yelled. "You mean you DIDN'T put me under a SPELL?"

"INSPIRATION?" I blurted. "And what's that supposed to mean?"

"It's funny you say that." Mother laughed. "I didn't think you would fill up the first one so fast. But just in case . . ."

"Just . . . in . . . case," Mother repeated, "I bought you THIS." Then she reached into her mermaid purse and pulled out a brand-new tortoiseshell DIARY!

I grabbed it and flipped it open to the first blank page. It was beautiful.

"SHELLFISHALICIOUS!" I screamed. Then I started writing.

Monday

Last night, all I wanted was a good night's sleep, so my mother told me a bedtime story. And I tell you, it was SHELLFISHALICIOUS! It even had **NARWHALS** in it! You know, the **UNICORNS OF THE SEA!**

But when I finally went to sleep, that's all I dreamt about! **NARWHALS swimming around with their big twisty horns!**

And that would have been GREAT . . . if I just stayed asleep! But halfway through the night, the craziest thing happened.

I woke up with an IDEA! It was for a story of my own (about narwhals, of course!), and I just HAD to write it down. I just . . . HAD to! Then I just HAD to draw pictures for it too!

Mother calls this "INSPIRATION" and tries to say it's a GOOD thing. But if you ask me, inspiration is the WORST thing to have when you're trying to sleep!

ACKNOWLEDGMENTS

An enormous thanks to my literary agent, **Dan Lazar**, for believing in Cora's voice in the first place. To my SHELLFISHALICIOUS editor at Scholastic, **Nancy Mercado**, who guided this story into more than I ever thought possible. To **Ellen Duda**, the magnificent **designer** who helped turn my quirky, **watercolor-splattered** pages into an actual book.

To my good friend **Ed Bloom**, who helped start me down this path in the first place.

To **Kellie Lewis**, who has helped and inspired me in more ways than I could possibly recount.

Thanks to Anne Bisson, Andra Oshman, Kristin Loboda, Brenda Allen, Mary-Kim Shurina, Keeley Lia, and a gigundo thanks to Adrienne and Jon D' Alessandro, Cindy Bohn, Rose Pollzzie, Cheryl Cassano, Michael Fiorito, Heather Butler, and Lisa Jones and the Osceola County Library system. Special thanks to Chloe Lafreniere, Tracy Russell, Janelle Bell-Martin, Chad Thompson, Nathan Greno, Jason Peltz, James Harris, Merritt Andrews, and Dominic Carola. Last but not least, thanks to my brother and sister, who never stopped believing in me.

About the Author/Illustrator

Peter Raymundo has loved writing and drawing since he was very young. Despite everyone always saying he couldn't get a real job by doing this, he never stopped.

Peter has worked as an animator on some of the biggest animated movies of all time, including *Mulan*, *Tarzan*, and *Lilo and Stitch*. He's also the writer and illustrator of several children's books, including the one you now hold in your hands.

In short, always follow your dreams. You never know where they will lead.